A BENEVOLENT GODDESS

ANITHA KRISHNAN

DREAM PEDLAR PUBLICATIONS

Ebook ISBN: 978-1-7752278-4-7

Paperback ISBN: 978-1-7752278-6-1

Cover stock image 'Dancing girl with red and bright ribbons' by YAYImages on Depositphotos

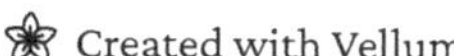 Created with Vellum

About This Book

A Benevolent Goddess

Countless gods you pray to. Only one answers. It will cost her dearly.

In a land where gods have long mastered the art of ignoring the prayers of human beings, a new goddess arrives. She desires nothing more than to help those who call out in faith.

But every choice, no matter how noble, comes with its own consequences. Even the benevolent goddess will have to pay a steep price if she chooses to follow her heart's desire.

For Minal
With a friend like you, I need not pray to any god, benevolent or not.

For Abhinav & Dhruv
The greatest miracles in my life. Love, always.

CHAPTER I

BEGINNINGS

In a land where they worshipped gods of stone and clay, the new goddess decided to rise from the belly of the earth and install herself halfway up the top of a mountain.

She went largely unnoticed at first, for the mountain slopes were steep and treacherous, snow came to rest on its peaks in the winter, and it wasn't until spring arrived and the people of the land could climb up and down from their village at the foot of the mountain to the ancient temple at its peak safely, without too many casualties, that someone noticed how the land had shifted, how the trees had parted, and how even the stream that sprung from the melting snow had chosen a little deviation, going just around that circular patch of grass and coming back to its original course, to hurtle down to the thirsty village and beyond.

And right in the centre of that circular patch of grass, which was a vibrant green and over which sunlight poured without any obstruction, as if even leaf-shadow dared not disturb the sacred space, stood a rather ordinary-looking stone. Dark grey.

Almost black. Smooth. With no jagged edges, so clearly it wasn't meant to be climbed upon.

It was quite long. Tall. As high as two men, one standing on the other's shoulders. Almost cylindrical, except it was curved on the top. Like a nail-less finger sticking out of the earth. Or a phallus, as some of the more discerning eyes observed but dared not say out loud.

It was also quite wide. Even ten men hugging it and holding each other's hands wouldn't have been able to encircle the stone.

(Of course, this was only a hypothesis, for no grown-up wanted to touch the structure without being permitted. By whom? The government? The priests? Aliens, maybe? No one really knew but the people of that land had become accustomed to living by rules that someone else made. And who knew what consequences would fall upon the miscreant who dared meddle with what was most certainly a supernatural phenomenon?)

Why the new goddess had chosen this shape was anybody's guess, but it took a five-year-old to state the obvious.

"It looks like a weenie," Leya said one day as she trotted beside her mother, three older brothers, and two older sisters up the mountain.

Her declaration brought everyone to a halt. Mother turned around and gave Leya an especially stern look. But her older sisters, seven and nine years old, burst out giggling. Her oldest brother, all of ten years old, who had trekked several paces ahead, came running back down and asked her, panting, "And how would you know what a weenie looks like, little sister?"

Leya put her hands on her hips and thrust her chin at her oldest sibling. "Of course, I know! I saw Simona's mother change her baby brother's diaper the other day."

The goddess, ensconced inside her humungous and solid house of stone, shook so uncontrollably with laughter that the earth around them trembled. Loose rocks and stones began to roll downhill.

"Run!" the mother cried, and for once all her children obeyed her command without pausing to argue or whine or pout.

The family spent the next few days recounting their adventure to all and sundry, narrating in great detail how the earth had first twitched under their feet for a brief moment, like a warning, before the rocks on her face had dislodged, as if unseen hands had begun to pelt them at the mother and her six children.

And wasn't it a miracle that they all managed to reach their home in the village at the foot of the mountain, their faces red and their lungs bursting from the exertion but with not the slightest scrape on any of their bodies?

What a benevolent goddess, the mother sighed, for it was she who had kept them from harm. What a benevolent goddess, everyone in the village began to say.

And as that story of the family's escapade was told and retold, as it was stretched and contorted to fit the shape of the mouth and the breadth of the imagination that formed it anew, everyone forgot the indisputable fact that Simona had a baby sister, not a baby brother.

And Leya, who was the only one who dared not recount their adventure, promised to never peep into her brothers' room ever again.

"You nearly got Leya into trouble," the gods who resided in the temple at the top of the mountain admonished the new goddess.

"But I didn't!" the goddess snorted. "She was such a peeping Tom. And now, look, she has mended her ways without being found out. I did her a favour."

"We're not supposed to meddle, you know that."

"Yeah, yeah! Way too boring."

Which seemed to explain why she had chosen a provocative shape, one that would get tongues wagging, eyes widening, and minds concocting mischief.

Occasionally, an official-looking person or two from the nearest town, several hundred miles away, made their way to the village to scrutinize the new structure. Often, they brought tapes and special equipment that they mounted on three-legged stands along with a thick air of authority, and took measurements and notes, conferred in private, then went back to their fancy town without sharing any of their observations and findings with the people of the village.

By the time they reached their fancy town in their fancy cars, the goddess transformed their meticulous notes into hilarious doodles and their mental observations into blurry images. So all they could show their official-looking bosses who bore even more pompous airs of authority were days spent in the sun on a circular patch of grass, dreaming and doodling.

It was all the goddess's doing, of course. She had come to help human beings. What sense did it make then to stay hidden inside a sanctum, where access was denied to those who needed it the most?

Soon enough, with all plans to erect a temple around the goddess shaped like a middle finger going awry, her installation became the haunt of wayward boys and girls, who preferred to be called young men and women.

Every evening, as the sun bled out of the horizon, bruising the sky in its wake, leaving behind wounds that the night sky quickly sought to hide, wounds that even a full moon would never reveal, these young men and women climbed halfway up the mountain and came to rest against the stone.

For that is all the goddess was to them. A stone. Hot to the touch under the afternoon sun. Cool as evening breeze under the gaze of the moon.

And they talked, and they smoked, and they made out. They had the most interesting conversations, it didn't take the goddess long to note. They talked about life and feelings, about their dreams for the future, their plans for themselves, and their hopes for the world. They smoked something that turned the air fragrant and made the goddess in her stone-house a little lightheaded.

Once, she reeled a little but then caught herself, not wanting to scare away these raw people, people who wore their feelings on their sleeves, young people who trusted their hearts more than their heads.

But they didn't notice her swerve, for they were under the influence of that thing they smoked endlessly, that thing which coated their lungs and slipped into their bloodstream and excited their brains.

And it made them look up at the stars and wonder who glued so many twinkling eyes to the night sky. It made them put their ears to the ground and swear they could hear the earth sigh and hum. It made them look into each other's eyes and swear they'd never look away, for surely now they had tasted all the happiness life could possibly offer them. It made them feel that this, right here, at the foot of this deity with the strangest of shapes, was where they had found heaven, and it made them wish that this moment would stretch and swell and fill up their entire lives.

The goddess felt all their longings as if they were her own, all the nameless things those young men and women yearned for, things she knew they'd never find in their homes or in their village, for these were unnameable things — you couldn't even call them *things*, for that matter, and gosh! how inadequate the language of words could be when one needed to describe that which mattered the most — but she felt them all the same, their heart's desires, how these yearnings twisted and coiled and uncoiled within those young bodies, clutched at their hearts, making them gasp at the immense possibility of it all, making them believe that the answers lay somewhere far, far away.

And she saw how their futures would unfold, how despite the promises they made to each other on these warm, summer nights, promises to never part, life would take them away and keep them away from each other. Like filaments of yarn, unspooling, unfurling, exploring a new way of being after all the time spent in being twisted and wound around each other.

She could have changed a few things here and there for them, but there were some things — that dratted word again, *things* — even she knew better than to muck about with.

And so she did what she could for now. As those young men and women lay against her, she took their pain and held it in her bosom, leaving in their hearts that raw optimism only young people seem to have, the kind that makes the aged envious of the youth. For now, that was enough.

CHAPTER 2

LONGING

But then summer slipped away, and autumn arrived without warning, and her visitors slowly ceased to come. Fewer and fewer people trekked up the mountain to the temple at its peak, the temple that was full of gods of stone and clay, gods who made no noise at all during the day and rested still as the dead, gods who turned a blind eye for they believed they were not to meddle in the affairs of the humans who prayed to them.

Even the sun did not linger. It ducked out faster than an eye could blink. And night came with great haste, leaving little room or time for a play of colours.

The goddess looked forlornly towards the western skies, sometimes wishing her young visitors would come again. But they didn't. Not that season. It had become too cold and too dark. And although the cold and the dark did not bother her, loneliness was a strange, new sensation the goddess had to learn to grapple with.

Disappearing into her thoughts became a habit. A matter of routine. Imagination, she came to find, was a wondrous tool. If she had been the one to create the world, the goddess thought during one of her jaunts into one of her many imagined worlds, she would have made her humans happier. Less afraid. More joyful.

The goddess wondered about leaving her stone abode and travelling through the breeze to the temple at the peak of the mountain. Visitors to the temple had dwindled. And the gods there, having committed themselves to remaining in that place of worship, were growing restless. Where they once stayed quiet all day long, they now stayed up all night, feasting and indulging in raucous, inebriated disputes. So loud they were she could hear them halfway down the mountain, although she knew that the sounds of gods would never fall on human ears, even if one were present right in their inner sanctum.

On one such sleepless night, even conjuring up happier destinies for the young lovers of summer who had frequented her abode could not help the goddess ignore the rowdy shouts and hoots of laughter that spilled down the mountain slopes from the temple at its crest.

Lured by the promise of something different, a balm for her lonely soul, the goddess left her abode and rode on the breeze to the temple at the top.

In the dark of the night, the temple's tiered, tapering roof glowed like a beacon. The humans believed that the roof was gold-plated but, in truth, it was the alchemical powers of the gods that transformed a mere structure of brick and mortar to present itself with such splendour. A silent light showing the way.

Inside, the place throbbed with music and conversation and laughter as the gods chinked glasses of nectar and danced to music that surely belonged only in the heavens.

Nostalgia bloomed in the belly of the goddess and gripped her so tightly she almost buckled over. The music was so famil-iar, yet she was certain she had never heard it in all the time she had spent in her stone abode on earth. But it was as familiar to her as her own being.

As if it were a melody she used to hum a long time ago, back when humans on earth could hear and enjoy and sway to the songs of the gods. But now the people could no longer hear the gods talk. And the gods who lived in this temple, the gods who lived on earth in some form, clay or mud or stone, they were not really gods in the truest sense, were they?

"Fallen gods." A god with four hands appeared in front of the bewildered goddess. He had a glass of nectar in each hand and held one out to her.

The goddess hesitated. She peered inside the glass. It had an exquisite shape, like a flower unfurling from a long stem. Inside, a liquid swirled. It had the purple colour of a bruised sky at sundown. It should have been thick as blood but was thin and fluid as water.

"It will help you remember." The four-handed god placed the chalice in her hand and drifted away.

The goddess stood for a moment, considering whether it would be wise to pour some of that liquid down her throat. She looked around at the other gods. Their faces were stretched into wide grins as they swayed and drifted. Their eyes were half-closed, as if whatever they saw on the inside of their eyelids was too bewitching and pleasurable for them to even consider opening their eyes and taking in the world outside of them.

And the goddess remembered her own joy, the delight that filled her being whenever she helped a human being. Whether it was keeping five-year-olds out of trouble or holding the raw pain of youth in her chest so their hearts could blossom with unbridled happiness, the very acts of helping and serving, guiding and nurturing had brought her alive in a way she hadn't felt ever since the leaves had begun to fall from the trees and the people had stopped climbing up the mountain. Instead, a strange chill had come to rest on the mountain slopes and clung to it like a shroud.

Well, the goddess said to herself, if a sip of the drink could make her happy once more, pluck her out of her loneliness for just a little while, that wasn't such a bad thing now, was it?

She took a tentative sip. Juicy sweetness exploded in her mouth and made her thirst for more. She tipped her head back and guzzled her drink in one greedy swallow after another after another, each gulp filling her with a giddy happiness that almost lifted her off her feet.

As the last drop slid down her throat and wound its way inside her, she pulled herself back upright like a reed in the wake of a careless wind and lurched towards the oblivious dancers.

And she closed her eyes and spun around, slowly at first, opening her eyes every so often to make sure she did not bump into the others. But she need not have worried. Every dancing god had been swept up into their own trance and had grown completely oblivious to the world outside them.

It took her a while, but the goddess soon grasped the steps of this inebriated dance. She held out her arms to her sides. And she turned and turned, she spun like the earth spinning on its own axis, worshipping its own self even as it circled the sun and paid obeisance to the source of light that kept life thriving on it.

And she remembered all that she had forgotten.

CHAPTER 3

NOSTALGIA

The goddess remembered her home in another land, a land of gods. They were called gods, yes, but they weren't gods in the sense that human beings knew. They weren't worshipped. They had no devotees. They were creatures, like any other. Some resembled human beings, yes, but only partly. Many had more limbs than could be counted. Many presented themselves in non-human forms.

She remembered her mother. Her mother had the face of a bird, the arms and legs of a human, the wings of an angel, and the tail of a fish. "So that I may take you to every corner of the universe," her mother had often said, she remembered now.

She remembered her father. A tall god with legs as spindly and sure-footed as a goat's and with the face of a lion. "So that I may keep you safe from harm at all times," her father had often said, she remembered now.

She remembered herself, as she had been in the land of the gods. A small being of stone. A stone that had been born with jagged edges and no describable shape. A stone that could barely be distinguished from any other, although her mother and father always knew which one their daughter was.

But very early on, she had discovered the benefits of inconspicuousness. She did not stand out, and she had discovered that she didn't want to either.

Instead she rolled and skidded and slid, discovering new lands and oceans. She went everywhere and no one ever noticed, because no one ever paid much heed to a stone unless it looked beautiful or had a distinguished pattern or hit them square in the head and drew blood from them. She crawled up steep mountain slopes, a feat that often took her weeks or months to accomplish. Twenty paces down for every pace up. And then she giddily rolled down on the other side, all the bumps and bruises no deterrent to the thrill she derived from her adventures.

Over time, all that rolling softened and smoothed her contours. And that was to her advantage, she found, for she could move faster, slip-slide with greater speed than ever before, and perfectly fit into nooks and crevices that had earlier been out of bounds to her once jagged edges.

Life was beautiful. Life was easy. Her very existence was full of the kind of stuff that mortal dreams were made of. Except, she didn't know that back then. She didn't know that human beings existed. She didn't know of the presence of life in any realm other than that of the gods.

She didn't even know there was anything beyond the beautiful paradise she had been born in, beyond the love and attention her mother and father showered on her and her siblings, the friendships she enjoyed, the adventures she had.

She didn't even have a name. No one in paradise did. No labels to distinguish one from another. They were all gods.

A long-ago ancestor of theirs had created the world they now lived in, and each new god that came took upon themselves to care for the land and preserve its beauty, to leave it a little more lovely and delightful for the ones who followed.

She was a young goddess. And her world was vast enough for her to explore without succumbing to boredom. Yet small and cosy enough for her to rejoice in the love and warmth they all shared no matter where she went.

Until she heard her first human call, and she had to make a choice.

CHAPTER 4

CHOICES

It was a sound the goddess had never heard before. A plea for help. Wretched. Desperate.

She had been rolling up a steep mountain that had not existed last evening but had suddenly emerged overnight. Especially for her, it seemed, as she woke up that morning and looked out of her window and took in the unexpected view of the new mountain that had sprung up in the horizon. A new place to explore, she had yelled out to her parents, and had run out of her house, lured by the prospect of yet another day of exploration and adventure.

She had climbed halfway up the mountain by late afternoon. No trails marred the face of the mountain for she was the first visitor to its slopes. She zigzagged between the evergreen pines and firs that stood so straight and grew so tall she couldn't help but stare at their tops, which yearned to kiss the white, fluffy clouds that drifted low enough but remained just out of reach, preferring the blue vastness of the endless skies to the green immobility of the towering giants.

The clouds were like her, she realized. A traveller. Always on the move. Meant to explore newer lands and horizons. And paradise, being what it was, offered her more and more of what she loved. New mountains to climb. New oceans to dive into the depths of. New skies to lie under. New stars to behold.

This was her fastest hike yet, she noted and thought with amusement that she would have been the perfect stone for Sisyphus to haul up the hill. Except, she would have rolled down on the other side and climbed back up herself, saving him the trouble whenever he needed to pause for respite.

It was this moment of unbridled joy that the strange cry interrupted. It came out of nowhere and flew right at her so unexpectedly that she fell back, as if struck, and rolled more than half the distance she had covered.

For in this land of gods, in this paradise, no one had to call out for help. No one ever fell in trouble — not in the way humans understand the word *trouble* — because no matter how tricky or unpleasant a situation any god might find themselves in, they always had the power to wriggle out of it. A flick of a wrist. A little spell. An arcane mantra. Everyone here knew the ways to keep themselves safe and happy.

When she came to a halt, wedged between a boulder and the trunk of a young maple tree, stunned, the voice called out again.

It said only one word. "Help!"

The goddess was spooked. It was the first time she had encountered fear in her life. An unfamiliar feeling. Although, the fear that had risen inside her and made her stone-body more rigid than it already was, had not been for herself but for whoever was calling out to her.

She zigzagged between the maples and the pines, the spruces and the oaks, trunks thick and thin, hoping the voice would call again if only to give her a sense of direction in which to proceed. She rolled this way and that, straining to hear the slightest sigh, the faintest whimper. She turned left, then right, then left again, trying to recall where the sound had come from.

But no matter which way she rolled, she realized long after, that the mountain was only leading her away from the cry for help. For she did not hear it again. And the next thing she knew, she had come to a halt right outside the door to her home.

She dashed inside, hollering for her mother and father. She didn't have to look long for them, for they had been waiting for her too, she could tell from the look on their faces, devoid of surprise.

"You heard it," her father said. It wasn't a question. He knew.

And she was the one with all the questions. "What was it? Who called out like that? What did they want? They needed help, but I couldn't find them. Could you please come with me? Help me look for them? A god is in distress and needs our help. Is that even possible?"

But her father did not budge. Neither did her mother. The young goddess searched their faces and registered their expression as sorrow.

But how could that be? How had she even known what sorrow looked like? Sorrow had no place in a land like paradise. Sorrow did not even exist, let alone have a name and a label and a set of facial and bodily expressions to go with it.

But she had known. She had remembered. Just as fear had assaulted her at first on the slopes of the new mountain, sorrow confronted her now, having taken up residence in the faces and bodies of her parents.

Her mother's bird-face cocked to one side, rendered askew by the weight of sadness. Tears shimmered in her beady eyes. Her father's lion-face was all sombre and droopy. Not so majestic anymore.

Their bodies had folded into themselves. Her mother's

wings and tails and her human limbs all pulled in, covering her chest and her belly. Her father's legs tucked under him, and he was no longer tall and imposing. He was at eye level with her.

It was almost as if they had had to contract themselves, stay put like a dam, to keep whatever grief bubbled inside them from exploding outwards and flooding their home and the land beyond, dragging all their loved ones in a raging torrent.

"You must make a choice," her father said at last. "You can pay heed to the plea. Or you can ignore it."

The goddess couldn't believe her ears. "Ignore it?"

"You must make a choice," her father repeated, ignoring her question. "No one can coerce you into choosing one way or the other. The choice is entirely yours. Whatever you choose, there will be consequences."

"What consequences?"

"You will not know until you have chosen."

"Then how will I choose?"

"You choose the way you always do."

The goddess stared soundlessly at her parents although countless thoughts whirred in her mind. What did her father mean that she ought to choose the way she always did? She had never given thought to her own thought processes. Until now, she had never had reason to inquire and explore how she thought, how she made choices and decisions. And now she had to.

So she thought back to all the times she had climbed up the slopes of mountains, old and new, strange and familiar. Every time she had come to a fork in the path, she had meandered wherever her heart desired. Left or right, it didn't matter. Perhaps one fork would have led her to her destination faster and easier than the other, but she had never felt compelled to make her choices based on ease and convenience. It had never been about reaching the top of the mountain. All paths led that way. If something tugged at her to take the path on the left, she rolled that way. For after her explorations down that route, she'd have another opportunity to take the trail on the right and see what it had to offer.

"But there is a catch?" the goddess asked, having discerned somehow that the choice she had to make was not as simple as choosing between two forks in a path.

Her father nodded. "You will see that the choice you make is irreversible. There is no going back."

No second chance to come back to the same fork in the path and make a different choice, try the other route, the one left unchosen the first time, if only so that she could tell herself that yes, the two forks in the path led through vastly different land-scapes, but no, neither could be labelled as better than the other.

But now she was being asked to choose without ever being permitted to find out what consequences the other choice would have entailed. Would that change how she made her choices?

"I must choose the way I always do?" she asked slowly.

Her father nodded. His face grew more contorted with pain. Her mother looked away. And the goddess had a feeling that no matter what she chose, the sorrow that was etched on their faces was here to stay.

She went up to her bedroom, somehow knowing it was the last time she would do so, and she looked out of the window at the new mountain in the distance.

Before the mountain had risen, she had had a view of a blue-green ocean that stretched all the way to the horizon. It was where the sun sank into burning waters every evening.

That morning, she had assumed that once she reached the top of the mountain, she'd find the ocean on the other side of it. Glimmering and glittering. Its waters all shades of blue and green, turquoise and teal. The late afternoon sun sprinkling his light on the waves, which would no doubt be devouring all his heat and light and reflecting a million shimmering jewels back at him.

But she hadn't even made it to the top. It was the first mountain she hadn't climbed all the way to the top. And it occurred to her that she may never be able to have another go at it.

But the sight of the mountain also brought back to her the call for help she had heard on its slopes.

It was a sound she had never heard before. A plea for help. Wretched. Desperate.

But it had also not been entirely devoid of faith. That is what she remembered the most now, as she stood contemplating the mountain and its mysteries. She already knew what her choice would be. She just hadn't known why, until now.

She ran back down to her parents. She did not have the heart to ignore a voice that carried so much faith and hope even in the kernel of its desperation.

"I choose to help," she said. "I choose to help," she cried louder. Her first utterance of these words having given her the courage to stick to her choice, her second utterance was an attempt at conveying the intensity of her conviction to her grief-struck parents so that they'd be proud of her choice.

But, if anything, her mother only sobbed louder, and her father bowed his head as if he wanted to not reveal how much more his face had contorted with pain and grief.

She rolled towards them, hoping for an embrace or a kiss, a few moments of bonding, a few words of encouragement before she set out to meet whatever lay in wait for her on this path.

But no. The instant she voiced her choice aloud, her world split into a before and an after. A then and a now. A moment ago, there had been possibilities. Now, in this instant, now that she had made her choice, all other possibilities were eliminated. She no longer belonged in this world, in this home with her father and her mother and her siblings, in this land of paradise with her cousins and relatives and friends and all the gods and goddesses who lived and loved here.

She had heard a call for help, and even the presence of paradise had not sufficed to distract her from responding to another being in distress.

She had not known it then, but it had been the call of a human being.

The trouble was that gods were not made to help human beings. Their paths were never meant to intersect. Not every god heard a human's plea. Those that did often chose to ignore it. It was the way it was. Something told them that to answer the call of a distressed human would put them in great peril. And they had learned to harden their hearts and sheathe their souls, for that was the only way they themselves could survive.

But there were a few like our young goddess, the ones who couldn't ignore a call for help, not because they were intrigued by the strange and unfamiliar cry, but because it triggered in them something raw, something so primal that it reminded them of the only timeless truth that existed, that every being, whether god or human or animal or stone, had emerged from the same source. They were all governed by the same laws of the universe. No matter how different they appeared to each other, they were all the same. And in each of them were embedded grief and joy, delight and despair, peace and conflict in abundant measure. One simply did not exist without the other.

And in recognizing that truth, the young goddess had stepped across the threshold that had long separated the land of gods from the land of humans. Before she could reach out to touch her father's face or her mother's wings, she was pulled back into an abyss.

She fell, the way her arduous climbs up mountain slopes often saw her rolling and sliding back several feet, quickly losing much of the ground she may have covered. Only, there was no way to climb back up.

She fell and she fell, and when she finally stopped falling, she found herself buried deep within ... she couldn't discern what it was at first. Loose, crumbly bits of what felt like mud with a rich scent that reminded her of the mountains she climbed. Cool and damp. And a darkness she had never seen before. Even the night sky on a moonless night had a certain pallor to it, a certain sheen from the distant lights of other celestial bodies. But this space around her had none.

She traversed through her terrain one way, she couldn't tell if it was up or down, but her surroundings became denser, harder, more difficult for her to press through. She turned around and tried to go back the way she had come but her path had been obliterated, the mud and the creatures that lived within it had quickly filled the gaps she had left in her wake.

Frustrated, she summoned all the powers and the courage she didn't know she had and pushed through, like an infant through a birth canal. Only, instead of travelling through and out, she grew. She grew and grew in size until she was large enough to break through the surface of whatever was pressing down upon her.

And when she emerged, she found herself halfway up the slope of a mountain, not unlike the countless mountains she had climbed up and raced down in the land of the gods.

And at first, she wondered if she had somehow arrived at the place where she had first heard the cry for help. The mountain looked eerily similar. Maples and pines, oaks and spruces.

But there was a certain orderliness to it. She couldn't quite place her finger on it, but something was different.

It was only when dawn crept up from behind the horizon and drove the night away, with way more force and swiftness than it gave the impression of possessing, that the goddess noticed the two anomalies of the place she had risen from.

There was a lot of death here, she was quick to notice. Trees whose trunks had shed their bark. Animals that killed another for a meal. Carcasses that disintegrated and seeped through the soil.

The other unusual thing was the abundance of human beings on this land. There was a certain routine to their movements, she noticed, almost a rhythm, but not the gentle, persistent lilt that other creatures displayed.

The rhythm of humans was replete with discordant sounds. Harsh words. Fear. There was a lot of fear. An ever-present worry of things going wrong, of doing the wrong thing, of life going all awry if they couldn't do what needed to be done.

The goddess had never experienced any of these emotions in her home in paradise, but she knew them all. She knew them as well as she had known her mountains. Every pain, every fear that touched the humans in this land, throbbed through her stone body too.

And the plea for help she had heard halfway up the new mountain in her home, in the land of the gods, the human voice she had chosen to respond to, had now drowned in a cacophony of cries and wails, each voice beseeching any god that would listen to grant them their wish. To protect them, to keep them safe from harm, to grant them prosperity and peace, to take away all their worries, to save them from death. Voices of the old and the young, voices of the weak and the strong, voices throbbing with joy and with sorrow, all merged into one constant hum, a drone just loud enough to keep even the weariest of gods from falling asleep.

The goddess cried for the very first time. In the bleak light of that first dawn in this strange land of human beings, she stood and shook, her stone structure trembled with heavy sobs as she cried for all that she had lost, and for all that she saw anew, which only seemed to reinforce her loss.

When the sun sailed up into the eastern sky and dried up her tears, she looked around her and saw the temple at the top of the mountain. She could sense the presence of other gods there but received confirmation of her suspicions only when she eavesdropped on the myriads of humans who trooped up the slope on a well-trodden path.

Gripped by an unexpected delight, she attempted to roll up the mountain. Only, she couldn't move. She grunted and twisted this way and that. Despite all her efforts, she did not budge an inch. For the goddess was no longer a tiny, loose pebble. No longer an ordinary piece of stone that could go unnoticed. That was the other thing she lost. Her anonymity. Her ordinariness.

In this land of mortals, she had been gifted a stature that commanded awe and respect. Attention, at the very least. She was now a large rock, a finger-shaped monolith, with a base buried so deep underground that movement was impossible, towering so high that she could converse with treetops at eye level.

People gathered around her and stared. Strange thoughts swirled in their heads but when they spoke, their words bore no resemblance to what they had been thinking.

And then a teensy human had come along and pointed at her and loudly labelled her a weenie. A phallus? Is that what she had become now? An object of jeer? Simply because she had chosen to respond to the cry of a human being, a human that could have been any of the countless two-legged creatures that climbed up the steep slope, bearing fragrant flowers and incense sticks and sweet fruits to bribe the gods in the temple, because they all sounded the same. Their whines and their desires were pitifully the same. Not a trace of imagination in their longings.

To lose in a single moment everything she had ever known and loved in a lifetime was too much even for a goddess to bear. And so she mustered all the panic and confusion — oh, such utterly human emotions — that had been gathering deep inside her ever since she had heard her first human call, emotions that had now morphed into fiery, spitting rage, and she let out a loud, anguished howl.

It was a caterwaul that did not penetrate human minds, so cluttered with thoughts and fantasies, but it pierced the ears of the gods who lay deep in slumber after a long night of partying in their earthly abode atop the mountain, ignoring the plaintive cries of their human devotees who never seemed to consider that their early morning pilgrimage up the mountain slopes took place at the most ungodly of hours.

And because the goddess's pain was so unbearable, so ludicrous, her tears dissolved into a manic laughter that the gods in the temple on the mountaintop had long come to recognize as the laugh of resignation. That moment when a god realizes how responding to a human cry had changed their life and all that they knew about it.

Fearing the destruction of their abode, one of the gods from the mountaintop temple rode on the wind, bearing a chalice of nectar in his hand, and splashed it on the goddess of stone. And she forgot everything that her life had been before she had fallen deep into this earth, like a seed, ready to sprout into her new form, her new life.

But the goddess's body-convulsing, heart-shattering

expression of emotions caused the earth she was trapped in to shudder and shake. Stones and rocks were dislodged from the seats in the soil they had occupied for decades.

Leya and her brothers and her sisters and their mother ran back to their village, abandoning the baskets of flowers and fruits they had brought to offer to the gods at the mountaintop temple.

But even in her moment of madness, the reasons for which she had now forgotten, the goddess had been able to keep Leya and her family from harm, and she had earned the reputation of a benevolent deity in the aftermath of her good deed.

She had held a grudge against Leya for a while. That child's insolent observation had caused the goddess to unravel. But the goddess soon observed that the child had been among the purer of the species. Prone to speak her mind. Truthful, in some aspects, even though she had been quick to spin a yarn to cover her tracks.

It wasn't the child's fault, the goddess had realized later. She had only lied because the people around her were incapable of accepting the truth that children are curious and that their physical forms are a source of wonder to them, not objects to be concealed and maligned in the guise of shame and morals. The goddess admired Leya's spunk. And so she had tinkered with the family's recollection of the incident, only a wee bit, of course, and had let them concoct the story that helped them cope with the trauma of an entire mountain slope threatening to give way under their wobbly legs.

And when the other gods at the mountaintop temple had chided her for putting an entire family at risk, wobbling the entire mountain with her uncontrollable tears and then manic laughter, the goddess had shrugged them off. She had blamed Leya for being a peeping Tom and knowing way too much for her age about boys' private parts.

But there had been no need for pretence. They had all suffered the same fate, the same losses, for having succumbed to the very godly desire to help, to serve, to ease the pain of a human being.

Only, the goddess had now forgotten her misfortune.

CHAPTER 5

CONSEQUENCES

Remembrance took effort. When the goddess came to, she was no longer spinning but it was the temple that spun around her. She was on the ground, a flat, smooth surface of cool marble, its lustre worn out by the relentless tread of barefoot devotees over the years. But there was a softness to it. A certain pliability the hard marble had come to acquire as it soaked up the faithful prayers of those who earnestly believed that the gods in this sanctum would ease their lives.

The music had long ceased to play. All the other gods lay on the floor, scattered. Each was cocooned in a pale white aura. Their god-essence, shining out of them when they dropped their guard in this state of inebriation. They looked like glowing orbs of light. As if someone had accidentally ripped a necklace of pearls and each bead had skittered away to the farthest corner it could find. Far away and out of reach. For never again would they commit the folly of helping a human being and lose even this camaraderie they shared, this group of sinners.

How easy it would be to stay here, the goddess thought. Now that she remembered everything, surely she'd need to forget and erase those painful memories over and over again. Drink herself to oblivion, like these gods in the temple did, and let every human prayer bounce off her, unheard, unheeded.

She understood their indifference now, their strict instruction to her to not meddle in the affairs of human beings. Knowing what she knew now, remembering all that she had forgotten, surely she too would never heed the call of yet another human being. Nor hold their pain, for it would only aggravate her own affliction.

But her abode was on the slopes of the mountain, not on its crest. She preferred the tilt of the land on a slope — upward or downward, whichever way you looked at it — to the jagged pointedness of the peak. She adored the transitoriness of a slope, and now she knew why, for it reminded her of her own countless journeys up and down mountains.

It also offered a vantage view of the very peculiar species of human beings who trudged up and down the mountain, carrying offerings and prayers for gods who cherished neither. She would never trade her stone home in for the aloofness of a mountaintop temple.

She cast one last look at her inebriated companions, then peeled herself away from the comfort of belonging to a tribe and made her way on the wind down to her home, that solitary oblong structure that belonged solely to her and to those un-godlike beings who sought refuge against it.

The downwind brought her back home faster than it had taken her to go uphill. But it wasn't until the goddess was back inside her stone home that she heard the cries that came from the other side of the stone structure, the curvy part that faced the village at the foot of the mountain.

And there, darker than the darkness around it, lay a shape pinned to the grass, writhing and struggling under the weight of another larger shape atop it.

The goddess took a moment to wriggle out of her inebriation and take in the scene unfolding in front of her. The cool air had strangely become warm and damp with the exertion of movement. It was thick with a sense of urgency. Fear held a stranglehold on it.

Pain punched the goddess somewhere deep inside her as the man on the ground pushed his way into the woman floundering under him. His grunts were louder than her cries, which he had muffled by a relentless press of his hand on her mouth. Large, thick fingers that crushed her nose and her lips, leaving her gasping for breath and words.

But her plea was unmistakable. "Help!" She cried, even though it was the faintest of whispers, even though she was screaming with all her might.

How could the goddess not help? She pulled herself up and let out a mighty roar, the collective sound of a thousand lionesses protecting their cubs from predators, and the world around them shook.

The man looked up, dragged out of his rapture, caught in that liminal state between fantasy and reality. His mouth hung open. His eyes were unfocused. But only for a moment.

For the next roar brought terror flooding into his eyes and his face. And a moment was all the woman needed. She bit his hand, his crushing grip of her mouth and nose having slackened momentarily. The pain drew his attention back to her, and he raised his hand and slapped her across her face.

Enraged, the goddess pulled herself up and roared a third time, a call for the earth under her to wake up, a call to all the boulders and rocks on the mountain slopes to come hurtling down and strike down this brute. And the earth responded to her.

At the sight of the rocks and boulders rumbling down the

mountain slope, the man jumped up, gathered his trousers around him, and ran down towards the village for dear life.

The woman was relieved at this turn of events, but the sight of the rocks hurtling down like an avalanche towards her brought another fresh wave of terror.

The statue of the goddess wobbled, and the woman worried it would topple over and fall on her. She got up, but instead of running away, something made her run towards the tall stone, the one that looked like a phallus. And the stone shuddered and split from the base up into two, but not all the way to the top, and the crack widened until it was large enough for a person to squeeze into. Like a mouth opening. Lips parting. An invitation to enter.

The woman looked up with wild eyes. All the boulders rolling down the mountaintop steered clear of the goddess's abode. And she knew what she had to do. She wedged herself into the crack and sat there, while the earth around her trembled and throbbed, shook and shuddered. As if something deep inside the earth had tired of being pressed down upon by layers and layers of rock and soil and human and animal treads for centuries and the burden had become too much to bear. Quite like how she had struggled under the weight of that horrible man and had wanted nothing but to throw him off.

And to think she had agreed to climb up the mountain in the dead of this almost wintry night. *The benevolent goddess will bless us*, the man had said, and she had foolishly believed him, completely misjudged his intentions.

A cold shudder ran up the woman's spine, and it had nothing to do with the earth collapsing around her. Sheltered within the dwelling of the benevolent goddess, the woman felt like a child deep inside the deity's womb. She was safe here. She was protected. But only a few moments ago, her life had been on the verge of utter and irreparable ruin. The thought gripped her and blanketed her in a chill she'd spend the rest of her life trying to shake off.

As if in response to her thoughts, the cave-like fissure in the stone grew warm and silent. The woman leaned against one wall and tucked her legs under her. Pieces of the mountain rolled down past her but within the safety of her cocoon, she no longer heard their thunderous descent. It was like sitting beside a warm fire on a cold wintry night, watching fat flakes of snow fall to the earth gently. The goddess was truly benevolent. The goddess will protect her. For now, she was safe.

THE GODDESS HOWLED AND HOWLED. She was privy to the thoughts and fears of the woman for whom she had split herself wide open. How could one human being inflict such pain on another? It was a conundrum she couldn't resolve, no matter how she twisted and turned it in her head.

The goddess wept. And the earth she had risen from wept with her too, shedding tears of rocks and soil and fallen trees.

The temple at the top of the mountain trembled and shook. For a long time, the inebriated gods inside remained oblivious to the turmoil in the world around them. But when the roof cracked and caved in, even the most intoxicated of the gods couldn't help but jump up, startled into consciousness from deep slumber.

But even as their earthly abode crumbled and crashed around them, even as they staggered and stumbled, forgetting to conjure up any powers they could wield to stop the storm raging around them, something shifted. One by one, they began to drift upwards. The earth, in the midst of her heaving and moaning and labouring, began to lose her grip on them.

The bricks and mortar that had constituted the temple

walls and roof for centuries crashed to the ground and slid down the slopes of the mountain.

Pale, white orbs of light drifted out of the debris and floated away into the skies, each fallen god no longer a prisoner in their home on earth.

Each god that had resided in that temple was now rewarded with a journey back to their true home in paradise. Each had learnt their lesson to never again meddle in human affairs, to ignore all pleas for help.

Only the goddess had failed to do so.

CHAPTER 6
LEGEND

A very long time ago, there used to be a temple at the top of a mountain. A temple that housed gods of stone and clay, many shaped like human beings but with some distinguishing characteristics to set them apart. Eight arms. The face of an eagle. Angel wings. A lion for a mount.

The people who lived in the village at the bottom of the mountain climbed all the way to the top, bearing prayers and offerings. Their prayers went unheard — of course, they would never have believed such a thing even if the gods they prayed to had dared confess their utter indifference to human woes.

Whenever life sent prosperity their way, they were quick to attribute their good fortune to their unswerving faith in the gods. Whenever misfortune knocked on their doors and took up residence in their homes, they blamed it on the temperamental nature of life.

And then another divine being had appeared on the slopes of the mountain. A faceless, nameless structure of obsidian stone. Blacker than the night. Shinier than any jewel anyone had ever seen. This one had the strangest of all shapes.

Despite the curiosity and faith she had quickly aroused

among the villagers — it was no mean feat to save a family of seven from a rockslide — her persistent resistance to having a temple or even some sort of a sanctum built for her had quickly turned her abode into a haunt for wayward teenagers.

She seemed to like them. Besides, they didn't get up to much more than the usual mischief in her shadow. Draw a little breath of something intoxicating into their lungs. Feed their young hearts with dreams of great ambitions and grand love.

Until that strange night, the night that was never forgotten, the night that was spoken of over and over again long after the village ceased to exist, the night the mountain came crashing down and almost buried an entire village and its people under it. *Almost,* because it didn't exactly decimate the village. All the rubble stopped sliding just short of the long line of pines and maples that separated the mountain from the farms of the village.

So when the villagers awoke the next morning, having slept through the commotion of destruction in their backyards, they found to their greatest astonishment that a new mountain had formed. It was larger and closer than the earlier one had been. But it also appeared as a huge pile of rubble. As if the earth had thrown up everything from the deepest part of her belly overnight and buried the slopes of the old mountain under it all.

Gone was the temple at the top of the mountain. Gone was the oft-trodden trail that led countless devotees to the temple of the gods. Gone was the new stone goddess.

A few brave people from the village attempted to climb the new mountain, but it pushed them back into the village even before they had taken five paces.

Over and over again, they tried. Over and over again, an invisible hand pushed them back. The message was clear. The mountain did not intend to brook any more people seeking to trample on her face.

That morning, a young woman emerged from a narrow cave on the side of the mountain, a cave just large enough for one person to take shelter in, a cave that appeared as black and shiny as the mysterious stone deity that had once emerged as a finger (or a phallus, depending on who you ask) in that very spot. No doubt, that structure too had now been devoured by the mountain turning itself inside out.

The woman ran down the mountain, slipping and sliding on the loose earth under her feet, the events of the previous night raging like stark memories in her head. Faster and faster she ran, trying to outrun all that had happened, desperate to erase every memory of it from her body and her soul in the days to come.

The goddess was a benevolent one. She answered prayers.

When the woman burst through the thicket of pines and maples that separated the mountain from the farms on the outer edge of the village, she forgot everything.

Remembrance takes its toll, the goddess understood. So she spared the young woman the ordeal of having to remember and relive that ghastly night every remaining day of her life. The goddess took her pain and buried it deep inside the cave.

When the woman left the mountain, she no longer had any memory of all that had transpired the previous night. She stumbled across the fields and made her way home. At the sight of her, her mother's heart exploded with relief.

The night in question, a young man went missing. He also went missing from the memories and recollections of every being that breathed in the village. No one mourned him. No one looked for him. No one even knew he had ever lived and breathed and laughed and celebrated alongside them.

And because nobody could gain access to the slopes of the

mountain anymore, no one knew that at the top of the mountain now resided a goddess. A small, round stone so ordinary looking no one would be able to tell it apart from the countless others that lay scattered around it.

She stayed there, filling her days with memories of rolling down mountain slopes in another world, of young love and of age-old betrayal, of wayward companions and this eternal loneliness.

There, on the peak of the mountain, where the winds blew hard and the clouds sometimes obscured her view, she could no longer hear any cries for help.

It was just as well, for she didn't know what she would do if anyone ever cried out for help.

Occasionally, she made a plea.

Sometimes, a whimper.

Sometimes, a holler.

Always, it was a single word.

"Help."

No response ever came forth.

Not even an echo.

~ THE END ~

AUTHOR'S NOTE

A Benevolent Goddess began in my head as a cheeky flash fiction tale on a quiet afternoon in late-January this year, when I was struggling to edit three other manuscripts — a full-length novel, and two novellas, which will be published later this year.

I have reached a stage in my writing journey in which getting to the computer to write is not as difficult as it once used to be, but my inner resistance surges wildly when it is time to go through the drafts, edit and polish them, get the covers designed, and make the books available for sale on various retailer websites.

Desperate for an excuse to procrastinate, I began to write a new story, expecting it to be no longer than 1,000-3,000 words. But the muse had her own plans, and the story took on a life of its own and became *A Benevolent Goddess*.

And now, instead of three works, I found myself holding four manuscripts to put through the publishing process.

Moreover, at just shy of 10,000 words, it was hard to categorize the tale in terms of length. Short story? Novelette? A *long* short story?

But it was precisely because of this short length that I

managed to edit, format, and publish it before my steadfast friend — procrastination — could talk me out of it.

So here we are. We've come together so far, and I hope you would like to stay connected with me.

I send out a monthly newsletter on the last Sunday of every month. Subscription is free. When you sign up, you will gain exclusive access to a free short story titled *Hide-and-Seek* as well as other short fiction available only to subscribers.

You will be the first to hear of any forthcoming works, including the above-mentioned three that spurred me to write this story. I will also include updates on my writing life, book recommendations, and occasional surprises.

Thank you for staying with me this far. If you choose to accompany me further on this journey, I promise you a magical ride.

Delightful dreams and wondrous whimsies. Impossible illusions and fleeting fantasies. Straight from The Dream Pedlar's emporium into your mailbox!

Climb aboard at https://thedreampedlar.com/newsletter!

~ Anitha Krishnan
Burlington, Ontario
26 March 2022

TO YOU, WITH LOVE

Writing has been such a solitary pursuit that in all these years I've somehow let slip from memory all those who shared my journey in some way or the other.

But as I craft this book to pass on to you, I am reminded that today is also the first publication anniversary of *Dying Wishes*, which was released exactly a year ago. So it seems a perfectly fitting occasion to recall, as many as I can, those who have helped me, knowingly or unknowingly, in my journey so far. I shall proceed chronologically.

Padmaja, you are the first who comes to mind. About 15 years ago, we became blogger buddies on a now-defunct Indian blogging platform, Sulekha, and we have remained in touch ever since. You have commented on every single one of my posts and watched me grow through my myriad online writing avatars. Thank you, dear friend, for your calm presence and constant support.

Shreyasi, you are the one I turn to for conversations on words and how they make us feel, as well as for conversations on feelings that simply cannot be put into words, yet you somehow understand. Thank you, dear friend, for being so close even though we are so far apart.

Minal, how should I address you? Friend? Sister? Nah! These labels do no justice to what you mean to me. I have no words to describe how much I cherish our friendship. You have been the bearer of light in some of my darkest times. You are the one who held the first print copy of *Dying Wishes* in your hands and spread the word to others. Thank you for your open-hearted generosity. I dedicate this book to you.

Abhinav, I've driven you mad for the past decade and a half with my talk of all things writing (and non-writing too). Yet, you stand by my side. I'm pretty sure you came into my life straight from the brightest stars. You remember all the times I used to tell you how I wish I could shrink and fit in into your shirt pocket? So that you could take me with you wherever you go? I still feel the same way even after all these years.

Darling Dhruv, I come to you right at the end but shall I tell you a secret? I dreamt of becoming an author for more than a decade, but it wasn't until you came into my life that I actually wrote and published my first book, *In Search of Leo*. For you, I want to be the kind of person who harbours a dream and works hard at it. For you, I want to be the kind of person who keeps at hard things, even if I end up failing. Thank you for coming into my life and changing my world.

~ Anitha Krishnan
Burlington, Ontario
26 March 2022

About the Author

Anitha Krishnan is a speculative fiction author and an award-winning poet. She lives in Burlington, Ontario with her husband and their cherished child.

Find more books and her blog on the writing life at
https://thedreampedlar.com.

Sign up to her newsletter at
https://thedreampedlar.com/newsletter
to receive exclusive updates, book recommendations, free
fiction, and more!

ALSO BY ANITHA KRISHNAN

https://thedreampedlar.com/books/

Dying Wishes

A contemporary fantasy novel weaving Hindu mythology and South Indian folklore into a quest for belonging across different worlds — the World of Mortals and the World of Gods, India and Canada, the past and the present, the world outside and the one within.

In Search of Leo

A tale exploring the gamut of emotions that loss and grief can stir.

Hello, Dreamer! Poems & Dreams

An eclectic collection of 100 short poems encompassing musings on the universe and its mysteries, nature and human life, my secret longings and fears, love and heartbreak, the sun and the moon, the stars and the seas, light and shadow, and joy and nostalgia.